This book belongs to

....

LADYBIRD BOOKS

UK | USA | Canada | Ireland | Australia | India | New Zealand | South Africa

Ladybird Books is part of the Penguin Random House group of companies
whose addresses can be found at global.penguinrandomhouse.com.

www.penguin.co.uk   www.puffin.co.uk   www.ladybird.co.uk

Penguin
Random House
UK

First published 2023
001

Licensed by

Printed in China

The authorized representative in the EEA is Penguin Random House Ireland,
Morrison Chambers, 32 Nassau Street, Dublin D02 YH68

A CIP catalogue record for this book is available from the British Library

ISBN: 978-0-241-60712-1

All correspondence to:
Ladybird Books, Penguin Random House Children's
One Embassy Gardens, 8 Viaduct Gardens, London SW11 7BW

PePPa
the Unicorn

One lovely sunny day, Peppa and her friends were having lots of fun playing in a GIANT muddy puddle. "Look!" said Peppa. "There's a rainbow in the puddle! It must be . . ."

Splash!

Squelch!

"MAGIC!" shouted Pedro Pony.
"We're jumping in a magic
muddy puddle!"
"We have to make a wish!"
said Molly Mole.
Peppa thought hard. "I wish . . .
I wish . . ."

Hee!
Hee!

Splat!

"Don't tell us your wish, Peppa," said Suzy Sheep. "If you do, it won't come true." Peppa whispered her wish very quietly to herself. "I wish I could be a magical unicorn!" Peppa had **always** wanted to be a magical unicorn.

All Peppa's friends thought hard and made their wishes, too.

Peppa was very excited when she got home. She **really** wanted to tell Mummy and Daddy Pig about her wish. Then she remembered what Suzy told her.
"Maybe I could just tell Teddy . . ." she said to herself.

So once George was asleep, and Mummy and Daddy Pig
had said goodnight, Peppa whispered her wish to Teddy.
"Today I made a wish that I could be a magical unicorn,
Teddy!" said Peppa.

That night, while Peppa was asleep, Mummy Pig
tiptoed into Peppa's room very quietly.

She put a unicorn horn on Peppa's head,
and then tiptoed back out again.

Tiptoe . . .
Tiptoe . . .
Tiptoe!

In the morning, Peppa came downstairs with Mummy Pig. Daddy Pig and George were in the kitchen.
"Good morning, Mummy Pig," said Daddy Pig. "Good morning . . . Peppa the Unicorn!"

"Daddy!" said Peppa, giggling.
"I'm not a unicorn. I just really
like unicorns!"
"I think you need to take a look in
the mirror, Peppa," said Mummy Pig.
Peppa went to see . . .

"I **am** a magical unicorn!"
cried Peppa, seeing her reflection.
"My wish came true!"
George giggled. "Hee! Hee!
You-ni-corn!"

Peppa told everyone about her wish. "I didn't
think I could actually **be** a unicorn!" she said.

"You can be anything you wish to be, Peppa,"
replied Mummy Pig.
"Dine-saw! *Grrr!*" shouted George.
"Yes, George," said Mummy Pig. "You can be
a dinosaur if you wish!"

"What do unicorns and dinosaurs like for breakfast?"
asked Daddy Pig when they were back in the kitchen.
"Pancakes!" said Peppa the Unicorn. "With fruit rainbows, please!"

"*Grrr!*" roared George the Dinosaur.
"I see," said Daddy Pig. "Fruit-rainbow, roaring pancakes coming up!"
Peppa and George giggled. "Hee! Hee! Hee!"

"So, how do unicorns get to playgroup?" Mummy Pig asked after breakfast. "Do they take the bus, drive, walk, unicorn-scooter . . . ?"

"No, Mummy!" said Peppa. "Unicorns FLY!"
"Of course they do," said Mummy Pig.

While Peppa the Unicorn flew, George the
Dinosaur stomped . . . all the way to playgroup.
"I LOVE being a unicorn!" Peppa cheered.
"I want to be a unicorn forever!"

GRRRRR!

STOMP!

When they arrived at playgroup, Madame Gazelle
answered the door.
"Oh, hello, Peppa the Unicorn," she said. "And hello,
George the Dinosaur."

Madame Gazelle didn't seem at all surprised that
Peppa was a unicorn and George was a dinosaur.
When Peppa and her family got inside, they
discovered why . . .

All Peppa's playgroup friends looked a bit different. Peppa saw that their magical muddy-puddle wishes had come true, too!

"It seems we have a few new friends joining us today,"
said Madame Gazelle. "I would like everyone to introduce
themselves. Peppa, you may start."
"Hello," said Peppa. "My name is Peppa the Unicorn. I love
rainbows, magic and flying all day with my friends!"

Everyone took it in turns to introduce themselves . . .

Molly was a
magical ballerina.

Mandy was a
magical shark.

SNAP!

SNAP!

Candy was a
magical witch.

Suzy was a magical octopus.

Pedro was a magical magician.

ABRA-CA-DA-BERA!

Can mermaids eat carrots?

Rebecca was a magical mermaid.

Gerald was a magical star.

GRRRRR!

Zoe was a magical princess.

And George was a dinosaur!

"Now, children," began Madame Gazelle, "as there seems to be lots of magic in the air, you can all go on a magical adventure in the playground!"
"Hooray!" everyone cheered.

Peppa the Unicorn and her magical friends zoomed around and around and around non-stop! They all loved magical-adventure playtime.

Later on, Daddy Pig came to pick up Peppa and George. "So, how do unicorns get home from playgroup?" he asked. "Wait! Don't tell me. They fly!"

Peppa the Unicorn was very tired. "Actually, Daddy," she said, yawning, "I think unicorns normally get a lift home."

"Dine-saw. *Ahhhhhh!*" said George the Dinosaur, yawning.

"I see," said Daddy Pig. "Well then, you'd better hop on!"
Daddy Pig carried the unicorn and the dinosaur all the way home!

After dinner, Peppa the Unicorn and George the Dinosaur got ready for bed.

"I loved being a unicorn and having magical adventures," said Peppa. "But flying was very tiring. Tomorrow, I think I want to be me."

"You can be whatever you want to be, Peppa," said Mummy Pig, taking off Peppa's horn.
"That's right," added Daddy Pig. "Today, you were a magical unicorn, but tomorrow you can be magical you!"

"Dine-saw. *Grrr?*" roared George the Dinosaur.
"Don't worry, George," said Mummy Pig.
"You can be a dinosaur again tomorrow!"
Everyone laughed. "Hee! Hee! Hee!"

Hee!
Hee!

Peppa loves being Peppa the Unicorn.
Everyone loves Peppa the Unicorn!